SPIDER MOON

Curse of the Gold Crescent

COLE TOWNSEND

Apple Publishing | 7056 Portal Way | Ferndale, Washington | USA | 98248 |
Telephone 1-604-600-6861

ISBN: 978-1-896817-51-4

1. Horror fantasy 2. Supernatural 3. Magical realism 4. Short story

Apple Publishing I 7056 Portal Way I Ferndale, Washington I USA I 98248 I Telephone 1-604-600-6861

The Amazon is the battleground where all living things must fight to survive. And for those who ignore her rules – it means certain death.

— Cole Townsend

To Ziggy

The assignment

A half-truth is the darkest lie – and as a reporter, I knew that better than anyone.

"Jebediah!"

I heard the boss yelling out my name above the clacking of typewriters, and the noisy chatter of a busy smoke-filled newsroom.

I reached across my desk and turned up the volume of my brand new Sony transistor radio which had just started playing John Lennon's latest hit, *'Imagine'*.

Catchy tune I thought, and leaned back in my chair to review the final draft of my resignation letter.

"Jebediah – there you are, boy – finish up whatever it is you're doing, and see me in my office," the boss demanded.

Bo Kingsly was my boss, and for the most part, we got along just fine – but when it came to news that was fit to print, we were miles apart.

I'm no Ivy Leaguer who went to J-School in Boston. I'm just a southern country boy who worked his way through Ole Miss. I said 'worked' – that's because cousin Orville's cotton plantation got swarmed by a pack of hungry boll weevils, and I lost my job, right along with the rest of the guys.

Truth be told, I never did graduate. Bo Kingsly offered me this job before I finished my final year – and with all the debt and student loans that were piling up, I jumped at the chance like a hound on a porterhouse. Bad choice.

"Be right there," I said, and stuffed the letter into the inside of my blazer pocket.

A steady paycheck was a welcome relief, but working at this place became a soul-sucking routine. Writing about Sasquatch sightings, UFO abductions, and giant swamp creatures was not the stories I wanted to be part of.

Those absurd headlines, the inane stories, the lies – right there in full display at every checkout counter, in every grocery store in America. They never seemed to bother Bo Kingsly, but for me, knowing my good name was attached to this trash was downright depressing.

I wanted to be a real journalist, a real reporter – and this place was definitely *not* the Washington Post. It's not like I had another job lined up, but anything was better than this, and so I was prepared to go it solo – ready to be a freelancer.

I slapped the wooden door frame of Bo's office twice and walked straight in.

"So, what's happening?" I asked.

Bo looked up at me and snuffed out his cigar. "I've got something for you, son – something I know you're going to like. Grab a seat, sit down."

I remained standing and reached for the letter in my inside jacket pocket. "Listen, Bo, before you go on, there's something I've got to—"

"In a minute, Jeb, hear me out. I just received a lead that could turn out to be the biggest story this paper has ever printed – and I want you to bring this one home to me. I want you to—"

"Let me guess, Bo – you want me to chase down another 'undisclosed source' who says they witnessed a woman drowning in her cake mix during the annual bake-off up in Michigan, am I right? Listen, boss, thanks, but I really need to—"

"Don't be a smartass, Jeb – now pull up a chair and hear me out. I'm giving you a chance to make a real name for yourself. Do you want to listen, or do I give it to one of the senior guys?"

I glanced down at the letter twitching between my fingertips and thought about simply handing it to him, but there was something in Bo Kingsly's voice – something different this time. What did I have to lose? I thought and decided to give Bo a listen.

"Lima," Bo said and unfolded a map of South America. "Here's where you'll start – right here in Lima," he said, tapping his finger on the map.

Lima? That caught me by surprise. I'd never been to Lima – never been anywhere outside of North America, and now Bo was going to send me to Lima? That got my attention.

"So what's happening in Lima?" I asked.

"There's been reports, Jeb – reports of a giant spider raiding villages in the Amazon – killing pets and livestock and attacking people too. The thing has a body the size of a bulldog – a bulldog with four-inch fangs and eight legs," Bo said, wide-eyed and looking quite serious.

I grew up near the banks and the bayous of the Mississippi River, and I've seen creatures of all kinds – bears and bobcats, hundred-pound catfish, and alligators the size of canoes – but never a spider the size of a dog. *Never*.

"That *would* make quite a story," I snorted, barely able to contain my laughter.

I was about to hand my resignation letter over to Bo when he shoved a photograph in front of me. It was a picture of a man – unshaven, with a broad mustache, and he was wearing an old steamboat captain's hat.

"Who's this?" I asked.

"That's Alberto – he's the one who gave me the heads up on the spider. He'll pick you up at Jorge Chávez International in Lima. From there you'll both head into the Amazon. He knows the jungle, like the back of his hand—"

"Whoah, hold up boss!" I had to think.

Bo sounded desperate. I knew this rag was losing subscribers, and just for a moment I admired Bo Kingsly for his tenacity – but was he offering me an all-expense-paid trip to the Amazon jungle?

I knew the Amazon was big – as big as the lower forty-eight US States combined. I also knew most of it was still unexplored, and that there were plenty of creatures running and crawling about. But a spider the size of a bulldog?

And just like the Amazon River, ideas began to flow. The Amazon just might be the way to jump-start my career as a freelance journalist, I thought. I could take plenty of pictures and submit my stories to real newspapers, and to magazines – maybe even to the likes of National Geographic.

There would be the giant *Kapok* trees, some growing as high as a twenty-story building and spanning ten feet across – and shirtless tribes, with blowguns and spears. There wouldn't be any giant spider with four-inch fangs, but there could be a Pulitzer in my future, I thought and smiled.

"Take a look at this," Bo said, and slid another photograph toward me.

The photo looked tattered and creased. I examined it closely and saw what looked like the remains of a deer, or possibly a goat. Whatever it was, the animal looked drained of all life, and guts – not much more than a hide draped over a skeleton frame. Poor thing must have starved to death, I thought.

"What's this?" I asked Bo.

"Look closer Jeb, look here to the right – over here by that bush," Bo said, hovering his pen in a circle.

I focused on the area Bo had pointed out and strained to look for something significant.

"That looks like it could be a—"

"Correct, Jeb, it's a spider – a very large spider."

That's not what I would have said. I could tell the photo was taken at night, and the area Bo had circled was grainy, and not much more than a confusing mashup of moonlight, shrubs, and shadows. Bo was seeing what he wanted to see.

But the idea of going to the Amazon excited me. It was a chance for me to put my talents to good use – a chance to advance my career.

Bo Kingsly leaned back in his chair. "Are you in, boy?" he said, relighting his cigar butt.

"I'm in, boss. You can count me in."

—

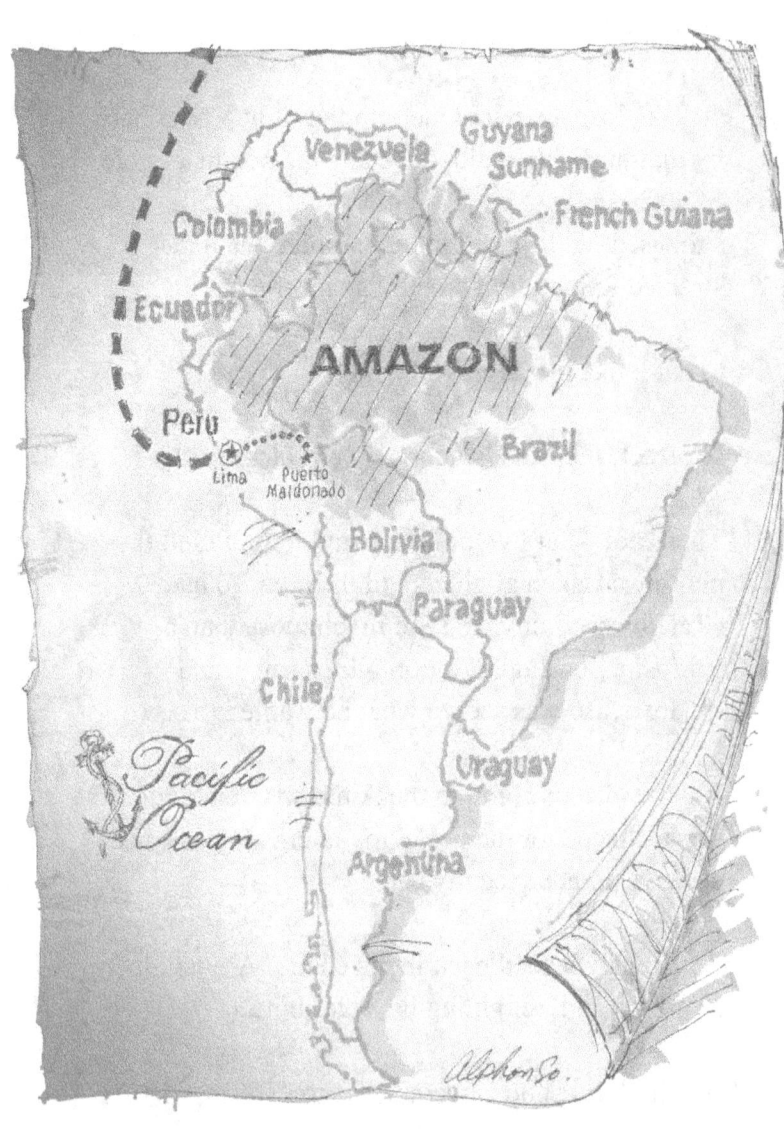

*The Amazon just might be the way to jump-start my
career as a freelance journalist, I thought.*

Welcome to Peru

"Ladies and gentlemen, we have been cleared for landing and will be making our final approach. Flight attendants, please return to your seats," a calm voiced announced over the intercom.

We began our descent into Lima, splitting veils of mist and white puffs of clouds. Through the window, I could see the majestic snow-capped mountains of the Peruvian Andes and their spectacular azure-colored glaciers.

The DC9 finally touched down, its tires skidding and screeching, its reverse thrusters howling. The plane slowed to a stop and the Captain welcomed his passengers to Lima.

I cleared customs and immediately started looking for Alberto. Within a few minutes, I spotted him, just outside the arrivals section, his eyes darting through the crowd. He was holding a sign that read, *"Bienvenido Jebediah."*

Alberto looked just like his picture – he was tanned and of medium build, with thick, black, finger-combed hair – his face unshaven, and sporting a thick mustache.

He was wearing a white shirt, the kind pilots wear, with button-down shoulder straps. The shirt was unbuttoned and splayed wide open, with the sleeves rolled to their elbows – the word *'Amazonas'* was tattooed along the length of his right forearm.

"Welcome to Lima, señor Jebediah!" Alberto said enthusiastically.

"Gracias, gracias – please call me Jeb."

Except for his accent, Alberto's English was almost flawless. We indulged in small talk and headed toward the exit signs of Jorge Chávez International, and out into a blast of hot and humid Peruvian air.

Alberto hailed a taxi and we scurried around the back of the terminal, toward a small cluster of hangars about a half-mile away. A man named Raoul would be there to greet us – the pilot of a single prop Cessna that would take us to Alberto's hometown of Puerto Maldonado – and to the very doorstep of the Amazon jungle.

Alberto and Raoul were friends and had flown many risky missions into the Amazon – often flying old and poorly maintained aircraft to distribute medicine, tools and emergency supplies.

The small Cessna lifted off a hot and sticky runway, and Raoul banked the plane steeply, and we headed east toward Puerto Maldonado.

Puerto Maldonado

Puerto Maldonado is a small city that sits on the edge of the Amazon jungle – an old city filled with quaint-looking shops, street vendors and noisy markets that haggle everything from fruits and vegetables to live exotic birds – to freshly gutted monkeys.

It was also our jumping-off point into the world's largest rainforest. From here we would travel to an undisclosed location into the village of the reclusive and fearsome *Toromona* tribe. Alberto told me it was there I would find evidence of the giant flesh-eating spider the natives called *'Ah-bee-too'*.

I checked into the *Wasai Hotel* and booked a room that overlooked the *Madre de Dios*, a river whose name literally means *'Mother of God'* in Spanish.

I unpacked my bags and laid out my camera equipment, and some old copies of National Geographic on top of the neatly made bed. This was my last assignment for Bo Kingsly, and I was going to make the most of it.

Alberto spent his day making sure the boat that would ferry us along the Amazon was stocked with food, extra containers of gas, camping supplies, a first aid kit, and plenty of drinking water. The journey would take several days and there would be no convenience stores or gas stations along the way.

—

The early morning sun was rising above a horizon of treetops, and I stepped out onto the tiny balcony, holding a toothbrush and a towel around my neck. I stood there and felt the cool morning breezes against my skin, and inhaled the sweet scent of jungle flora.

I could hear the haunting calls of macaws in the distance, and spotted a green cloud of parakeets – a flock of maybe a hundred birds, zooming and darting, and changing direction in perfect unison above the mangroves.

I gazed at the low-lying mist that hovered mystically above the *Madre de Dios* and watched as it melted away in the sun's warm glow.

Looking downward I noticed a boat and could read the word *'Mariana'* painted on its side. Alberto was busy making final adjustments on the heavily-laden vessel that sat tethered, waiting – floating peacefully along the bank.

It was a wooden boat, about twenty feet in length – her deck jam-packed with supplies, all neatly covered with an array of canvas sheets and bundled by webs of cord.

The riverboat looked sun-bleached and weatherworn, and a bluish-colored Johnson outboard motor jutted off her rear. Could've used a coat of paint, I thought. But the *Mariana* looked sturdy enough.

A Stowaway

I climbed aboard the *Mariana* and began to organize my belongings. Through the corner of my eye, I noticed a section of tarp moving and heaving slowly – as if something alive were underneath.

*Sloths are excellent swimmers, and can hold their
breath for up to forty minutes underwater.*

I lifted the tarp and found myself face-to-face with the strangest looking animal I'd ever seen.

A hairy creature, the size of a large housecat, with long ape-like arms tipped with three curved claws – and it was moving toward me, *very, very slowly.*

I jumped back, pointing downward. "Alberto, what the hell is that thing?" I shouted.

"What the hell is what thing, amigo?"

"There's some kind of furry space creature coming out from under the tarp – coming straight for me!"

"Oh, him, that's Pepi – he is a sloth, amigo. Pepi does not move fast, but he likes to go everywhere I go. He is my friend and he wants to be your friend too. Sorry, señor Jeb, I forgot to tell you."

Pepi was slow, but he was kind of cute, I thought.

Pushing off

The early morning temperature was beginning to climb, right along with the humidity. We wasted no more time in pushing off.

*The Amazon seemed raw and untamed, yet elegant
and graceful as the stork that glided silently past us.*

Alberto pulled the cord on the old Johnson two-stroke, and on the third attempt the engine began coughing and sputtering, and finally igniting – filling the air with clouds of smoke, and sounding like an angry chainsaw.

Pepi, Alberto and I slipped into the gentle flow of the *Rio Madre de Dios* and headed eastward toward the murky waters of the Amazon River.

Morning light is the best light for taking pictures, and so I began to unpack my camera. I put a fresh set of batteries into the Nikon and inserted a new roll of film.

It was like a new world to me – new sounds and things I'd never seen before surrounded me, and for a moment I forgot the reason for coming here.

I stood with my camera and began taking pictures of an endless shore of lush green forest, and exotic birds and plants that slowly paraded past us, as we pushed our way forward.

On the far bank were clusters of delicate butterflies fluttering bravely above the armored heads of black caimans that lounged lazily in the warm sun – their teeth bared like daggers.

The Amazon seemed raw and untamed, yet elegant and graceful as the white stork that glided silently past us – an enigmatic mix of beauty and savagery.

Alberto stocked the *Mariana* with the Amazon's abundance – avocados, bananas and figs, Brazil nuts and cashews, and acai berries – and plenty of *Cecropia* leaves for Pepi, by far his favorite food.

We had far to go and so we would snack on the run, slowing only to top up the engine's gas tank with the extra containers of fuel that we had on board.

A steady five mile an hour current, pushing its way toward the Atlantic Ocean helped the *Mariana* cover a lot of distance. The moon would soon be full, and there was no time to lose.

Breaking for Camp

It was a long day, and the sun had set behind the forest canopy. We traveled almost one hundred miles and the forest floor was getting dark. It was time to break for camp.

Alberto picked up the boat's powerful spotlight and scanned the shoreline for the perfect landing. The noise of the engine fell silent, and we drifted slowly forward, and the wooden hull scraped its bottom onto the sandy shore. For a moment, Alberto and I sat still and soaked up the welcoming quiet.

Pepi slept through the entire journey and was just now opening his eyes. Alberto climbed his way forward, and collared the strange-looking creature, tethering it securely to the hull.

We carried our supplies up the embankment, and Alberto began to inspect the lay of the land – carefully checking, under rocks and shrubs, and along the barks of trees.

I lit the Coleman lantern and began digging a small shallow pit, about twenty yards from the river's edge. Alberto didn't forget a thing, including a twenty-pound bag of charcoal. I tossed a few briquettes into the pit and doused them with some kerosene from the lantern.

The coals soon glowed red and I covered them with a few well-placed rocks. I wrapped two unpeeled potatoes in palm leaves as Alberto had shown me, and carefully placed them on top.

I unpacked the two fillets of salted fish Alberto had purchased in Puerto Maldonado just yesterday and laid them out on a paper plate. Fish and chips, Amazon-style, I thought.

Alberto finally returned, his fist clenched tight. He was holding onto something, *very tightly.*

"What took you so long – what the hell were you looking for back there?" I asked.

Alberto stretched out his hand and opened his fist. "I was looking for these," he said.

Damn, those were the biggest ants I'd ever seen – twice the size of anything back in Mississippi.

"Take some, señor Jeb. Put those in your hand and rub them on your arms – on your neck, too, like this. Rub quickly, or they will sting you."

"Sting me – are you out of your mind?"

"These are bullet ants, señor Jeb. Every living thing in the Amazon jungle is afraid of the bullet ant. When you crush them like this, they begin to smell, and the smell travels far – even the jaguar runs in fear when he smells the *Tocandira.*"

The Mississippi River was my playground, but this was Alberto's backyard, and so I took his advice. I picked up the remaining ants out of his hand and started rubbing them on my forearms and neck. I didn't want to be on some jaguar's menu.

"Your English is pretty good, Alberto – where did you learn to speak so well?" I asked, turning the potatoes over with a stick.

Alberto said he migrated to the United States from Ecuador when he was just sixteen. He entered illegally but managed to get a job as a mechanic's apprentice at a small airport outside of El Paso.

He learned to repair and maintain engines – the Piper, the de Havilland, and the Cessna 172. He loved being around airplanes, and pilots would often take him on trips, and he soon learned to fly.

All that changed when a zealous posse of Texas Rangers raided the small airfield, looking for evidence of drug smuggling. None was ever found, but Alberto was undocumented and was soon deported.

"In Peru, you work twice as hard for half as much, señor Jeb. The workdays are long here, and the pay is little," Alberto lamented.

"How did you come to know Bo Kingsly?" I asked.

"I was a big fan of your newspaper in El Paso. I read it often, and it helped me with my English. When I found out Mr. Kingsly paid for stories, I decided to try. Your boss liked my leads, and señor Kingsly always payed me well."

"And the spider story – is it real, or did you just make it up for the money?" I asked, grinning.

"The spider *is* real! I called your boss last week and told him so, and I sent him the photograph I bought from a homeless drifter. I would not have come this far if there was no spider, amigo."

Spider, or no spider – I've come pretty far myself, and one way or another, I wouldn't be leaving the Amazon without a story, I thought.

I handed Alberto a plate of salted fish and placed a well-done potato on it with the end of my knife. "What do you know about the spider?" I asked.

"I have seen the bodies – bodies drained of blood and body fluids. He attacks with black hollow fangs that sends poison and kills quickly and turns the insides into soup – it is the soup he likes," Alberto said calmly, chowing down on his dinner.

We talked about many things that evening. Alberto showed me a picture of his wife Maria. She was the love of his life and he named his boat after her.

She passed away suddenly nearly two years ago, and he couldn't afford a proper burial. He marked her gravesite with only a simple white wooden cross, and inscribed the words, '*Mi Dulce Maria*' in Spanish – my sweetest Maria.

He would visit her gravesite every Sunday and lay twelve roses on the ground beside the cross, and vowed that one day he would have the money to build her a shrine – a beautiful white marble headstone, sculpted in her exact likeness.

"How did you come to know the *Toromona*?" I asked Alberto.

Alberto explained how he was forced to make an emergency landing while flying supplies to a government outpost. He spotted a clearing about a half-mile from the River's shore and prepared the single engine plane for an emergency landing.

The plane's undercarriage caught the towering treetops and the Cessna careened out of control, landing upside down in the dense undergrowth.

Alberto and I talked about many things that evening
– Including a giant flesh-eating spider.

There was no fire and Alberto escaped with cuts and a badly broken shoulder.

Only minutes passed when the *Toromona* appeared out of the thick shadowy forest. Alberto had flown many missions and known many tribes, but he had never encountered the *Toromona*.

"They appeared from nowhere – a half dozen men carrying spears and machetes – out of the shadows, moving toward me like ghosts," Alberto said.

The men from the forest hovered above him – their spear tips pointed to within inches of his neck and chest, their machetes raised high.

He lay on his back and looked upward at the silhouetted shapes that encircled him, and thought of Maria, and that he would soon be with her.

But it was not Alberto's time to die. The tribesmen felt pity for the injured man who fell from the sky. They helped him to his feet and escorted him back to their village.

Alberto immersed himself in their language and culture while his shoulder healed. The villagers followed him whenever he visited the plane and watched in fascination as he made vain attempts to fix the plane's radio and location transponder.

Each trip to the crash site turned into a scavenger hunt for the children, who would frolic in the underbrush and find strange objects that once occupied the plane – an axe, a Zippo lighter, a broken wristwatch – and a first aid kit which contained small containers of antibiotics.

The *Toromona* numbered about two dozen and were a fierce and stealthy tribe – preferring hunting over farming. Even the illegal loggers gave them a wide berth to avoid a deadly confrontation for encroaching on their land.

Alberto explained that the *Toromona* called the giant spider *Ah-bee-too* – a name that means *'black hollow fang'* in their language, and that the creature hunted only at night, and only during a full moon.

He told me that the tribe's Chieftain wore a strange crescent-shaped necklace during special ceremonies – a necklace made of pure gold, and fringed with four-inch, black hollow fangs. The *Toromona* believed the sacred necklace had magical powers, and that it protected them from the deadly spider.

I flicked my cigarette into the dying embers of the fire pit. Tomorrow would be another long day on the river, and it was time to catch up on some sleep.

A Green Python

I awoke to the sound of a soft, warm rain gently tapping on the giant palm leaves hovering above my Head, and noticed Alberto kneeling beside the boat, and he appeared to be feeding Pepi. Alberto heard me stirring and turned toward me, pointing his finger and motioning me to look upward.

"Amigo, above you – look up there!"

I turned my head and did my best to focus on a tree that was only a few yards away, and saw something moving. It was bright emerald green and coiling itself very slowly around a thick branch that strained and bowed under its weight.

A surge of panic struck when I realized I was looking at a snake – a huge python, with a body as thick as my leg. Its triangular-shaped head was arched and pointed straight toward me, its eyes motionless, staring – its black tongue flickering, and tasting the air.

31

"What the hell happened to your bullet ant theory?"
I shouted at Alberto, leaping to my feet.

"That only works for eight hours, amigo – less
when it rains," Alberto laughed. "The snake does
not want you – he was after Pepi. Pick up your
things, we must get to the *Toromona* before dark."

Pink Dolphins

A long, narrow dugout sputtered slowly toward us.
It was loaded with produce, a few chickens and a
goat. A small family of indigenous villagers waved
to us as they passed – no doubt on their way to sell
or trade their goods with a friendly neighbor.

It was hard to believe that these winding shores of
endless bayous and mangroves, and almost
impenetrable forest, could be home to thriving,
human inhabitants.

"Look, amigo, over there – over to your right!"
Alberto shouted, pointing.

The river ahead was churning with a dozen or so
dolphins, diving and surfacing – an unmistakable
pod of pink dolphins.

I reached for the Nikon and shot a series of pictures in rapid succession, before the animals submerged for good beneath the murky water.

Alberto cranked the steering handle, and the Johnson motor revved loudly. He knew we would have to pick up the pace if we were going to reach the *Toromona* before dark.

The *Toromona* had no way of knowing we were coming, but they would certainly be waiting for us. They would observe the subtle changes in high-flying birds and listen to sounds of insects, and the howling of monkeys – all would tell them we were coming, long before our arrival.

The Toromona

We covered almost as much distance as we had the day before. Alberto idled the engine, and unfolded a hand-drawn map from his shirt pocket.

"We must turn off the main river, here," he said, pointing his finger on the map.

We were close to our destination, but the next few miles would be slow. Alberto steered the *Mariana* in a northeast direction, through a maze of channels

*The channels began to narrow, and Alberto slowed
the Mariana to barely a walking pace.*

and mangroves – passing strange looking trees covered in moss and their roots exposed, and dripping with vines that hung like ropes.

We glided slowly over the glass-like surface of the amber-colored water, and saw floating clusters of giant lily pads, some over six feet across – and the black caimans that submerged beneath them as we approached.

"Here it is, amigo!" Alberto shouted.

He found the landmark he was looking for, and from that point on, we would have to proceed with extreme caution. We had entered the back yard of the *Toromona*.

The channel narrowed, and Alberto slowed the *Mariana* to barely a walking pace. I could hear the loud guttural bellowing of howler monkeys echoing throughout the canopy – they were warning the *Toromona* that we were near.

We made our final turn and Alberto knew the *Toromona* would be waiting, invisible in the shadows and armed with bows and spears, and razor-sharp machetes. We were trespassers now, and Alberto could only hope they would recognize him in the dimming twilight.

Alberto shut the engine and the *Mariana* drifted silently forward. He scrambled to the front of the boat and stood on top of its wooden deck, and cupped his hands around his mouth, and began to shout out words in a language I didn't understand.

There was no reply.

The jungle was eerily quiet and still. The croaking of frogs and chirping of birds and the chattering of the squirrel monkeys had fallen silent.

Alberto shouted out again.

Still nothing...

The *Mariana* drifted aground onto the sloping shore, and its hull heaved upward. Alberto stepped into the water and whispered for me to pass him the large metal cooking pot from under the canvas.

The pot contained several smaller pots, some metal spoons and forks, a spool of fishing line, hooks, and a tin of coffee beans.

Alberto placed the pot on the embankment. He cupped his mouth and shouted out again in several directions. Finally there was a movement to our left along the forest's edge.

A half dozen shirtless men, with grim painted faces, began to emerge – stepping slowly and deliberately, moving silently like ghosts, and holding spears arched high and bows at the ready.

Alberto began to shout in their direction, and the men drew closer. The group's leader raised his spear, ordering his men to halt, and paused to focus on Alberto, standing there in the dimming twilight.

Neither man moved or spoke.

The leader slowly lowered his spear and a smile broke across his lips, and he extended his hand toward Alberto. The men began to exchange greetings, and the others gathered around – their threatening demeanor had all but vanished. They had remembered Alberto.

I leaned back against the hull and exhaled slowly.

After a few moments of laughter and friendly banter, Alberto returned to the boat, smiling. "They are going to take us to their village. Take with you only what you need, amigo."

Pepi was awake now, and Alberto secured him to the hull, leaving him plenty to eat. He reached for the slated wooden box of fruits, nuts and berries he had brought for our journey and set it on the shore, telling the men it was theirs to share. I grabbed my canvas backpack that contained the Nikon, and my new Polaroid camera I'd just bought back in Jackson, and we followed the tribesmen into the shadows of a darkening jungle.

We entered a small village compound and a small group of children and adolescents swarmed around us, and Alberto greeted them all, calling them by their names. The rest of the villagers smiled and waved, and watched us as we made our way toward the Chieftain's hut.

The camp seemed a happy place and I instinctively lifted my Nikon and began snapping pictures in rapid succession. The flash of the camera surprised the villagers, and some looked upward toward the sky, and others looked behind and into the trees.

Alberto ordered me to stop photographing, and began to vigorously apologize to the villagers, and attempted to explain what they had just witnessed. As he spoke they began inching their way cautiously toward me, and the strange-looking box that was strapped around my neck.

I reached for the Polaroid in my backpack and walked over to a brightly-colored flower, boldly protruding from a nearby bush. I pressed the shutter button, and the flash lit up the entire plant. The camera made a whirring sound, and a small four-inch square sheet catapulted forward.

I stooped and handed the picture to a child standing next to me. The little girl's eyes grew wide as a picture began to appear, and she turned and ran toward her mother, waving the picture wildly.

Her mother gazed at the rose-colored flower and was speechless, and a small crowd gathered behind her and peered over her shoulders, and marveled at the magical transformation.

The tribe's Chieftain emerged from his hut and asked to see the Polaroid picture that was being passed around. He looked at it only briefly before turning his eyes toward Alberto. His furrowed brow began to fade, and a soft smile came across his lips.

His face bore the look of someone who had seen much in life, his dark penetrating eyes seemed clear and focused – he was a serious, composed man, and had a quiet dignity about him.

The Chieftain's memory was long, and he recalled how Alberto had administered medicine to his people after his own efforts had failed to cure them

The Chieftain was a serious, composed man, and had a quiet dignity about him.

from an unknown illness – medicine from the metal box that the children found near the plane wreckage almost two years before.

Alberto was grateful too. The *Toromona* was not a water-faring tribe, but the villagers helped him build a raft and supplied him with food and water that would last three days.

He could navigate his way from their encampment, and float with the River's current, and reach the government outpost some ninety miles downstream – and return home to his beloved Maria.

The Chieftain ordered the villagers to prepare for the evening's ceremonies, and invited Alberto and me into his hut, to reminisce and share in a bowl of warm *Cauim*, a type of beer made from a fermented root – and discuss the nature of our visit.

Alberto and the Chieftain talked about the past and assured him that we were there only to take pictures and that the Tribe's location would never be revealed. The Chieftain trusted Alberto, and escorted us outside to a communal thatched hut and assigned us each a hammock.

Tonight there would be a full moon that would last three days, and the *Toromona* were preparing for the first of a three-day ceremony – a ceremony that would connect them with the spirits of their ancestors – and protect them from the deadly fangs of *Ah-bee-too*.

The Obelisk

The tribe's Matriarch was a handsome woman – her face adorned with red and white markings made from berry dye and liquid chalk stood at the doorway of the Chieftain's hut.

It was time to begin the ceremonies.

The Chieftain retrieved an object wrapped in a black satin-like cloth and placed it in the Matriarch's hands. Alberto knew what was under that cloth. He had witnessed many ceremonies while living with the *Toromona*.

He knew that the black shroud contained a crescent-shaped medallion made of solid gold and fringed with black hollow fangs. He also knew that the necklace was very old, and that the *Toromona* considered it to be sacred, and that it protected them from the bloodthirsty fangs of *Ah-bee-too*.

Was this the necklace Alberto had told me about? Could it be true – could the giant eight-legged creature really exist? I was getting intrigued.

The sun was setting behind the forest palms and there was a sense of mounting excitement throughout the encampment. Tribal women were moving about, lighting torches dipped in beeswax.

Men paraded in single file holding large wooden posts, and slowly raised their knees and stomped hard into the dusty earth while smashing their wooden battering rams into the ground.

There were musical sounds made with hollowed-out sticks, and children pranced happily about, their faces and bodies decorated with markings.

The *Toromona* no longer feared my camera and often posed and smiled for me. The revelry continued until the village Chieftain emerged from his hut wearing a headdress of colorful feathers. It was time to enter the sacred ground.

The village Matriarch led the procession carrying the sacred necklace in outstretched arms. The Chieftain followed and the children were next. Behind the children was a young mother holding her newborn, and behind her, the remaining tribe.

In the center of the clearing stood a four-sided obelisk, carved and polished from a marble ledge.

A short procession through a curtain of the thick forest led to an open clearing. In the center stood a six-foot obelisk, mysteriously carved out of a marble ledge – its four polished sides glistened in the light of a full moon and a dozen flickering torches.

The Chieftain kneeled before the strange sculpture, and the tribe's Matriarch clasped the gold crescent necklace around his neck. The village leader stood, his hands and eyes raised upward and began to recite his prayers.

The Matriarch lifted a wooden bowl, and each member lined up to sip a powerful concoction made of herbs and plants – a recipe passed down for generations that would make the villagers sleep and connect with their ancestors who would give them wisdom – and protect them from *Ah-bee-too*.

The prayers and celebrations came to a close and it was time for the villagers to return to their huts. Soon the entire village would be fast asleep, and in a dream state that I could barely imagine.

Alberto thanked the Chieftain for his hospitality and for allowing us to witness the sacred prayers. It had been a long day, and Alberto and I retired to our hammocks. It wasn't long before I was fast asleep.

An abrupt change of plans

"Wake up, get up now," I heard a voice say softly.

It was Alberto, his eyes were wide and he seemed distressed. "Pick up your things," he whispered. "We must leave immediately!"

I looked at my watch and saw it was just after midnight. "What's going on?" I asked.

"Quiet, we have no time. Come now, or I leave without you – move quickly."

Something was wrong, but Alberto sounded serious. I reached for my backpack and followed Alberto into the moonlit night, out toward the path that led us to the compound.

Alberto turned his flashlight on and we picked up the pace. Soon we arrived at the clearing where the *Mariana* was moored on the sandy shore.

He pushed the boat's hull away from the bank and climbed aboard, and quickly made his way towards the engine. "Get in!" Alberto commanded and pulled twice on the engine cord. The Johnson ignited and he reached for the large spot lamp, and aimed it in the direction from which we came.

We traveled for almost an hour, and no one spoke. Alberto slowed only to shine a light on his map and scan the waterway for landmarks. The channel gradually widened and we finally reached the River, and the wide-open moonlit sky.

Alberto seemed more relaxed. "We go west for an hour, then we break for camp," he shouted.

I was too tired to reply. I had all the pictures and excitement I needed for one day. Pepi was sleeping as usual, and I decided this was a good time to join him in a little shut-eye.

The fear itself

The constant drone of the Johnson two-stroke fell silent, and I immediately awoke and saw that we were drifting toward the River's bank.

I looked at my watch. "It's 2:30 in the morning, where are we?" I asked Alberto calmly.

The boat's hull rested on the sandy shore. "We will camp here and get some sleep – at daybreak, we head for home, amigo."

"What's the sudden rush?" I asked Alberto

Alberto reached inside his backpack and pulled out something wrapped in a dark cloth. He unraveled it, and exposed a crescent-shaped metallic object, and clasped it around his neck.

"How do I look, señor Jeb?" Alberto asked.

It was the sacred gold crescent – the same one that the Chieftain wore at the ceremony just a few hours ago. The yellow-colored necklace sparkled in the light of the moon, almost as if it were on fire.

"We need to go back now – you need to return it to the village. I won't let you do this!" I shouted.

Alberto reached into his canvas bag and pulled out a revolver. We are not going back, amigo."

"The spider, Alberto – the women, the children – what about the spider?

"There is no spider, amigo – it is just superstition. I have never seen the spider because he doesn't exist.

I made up the story for señor Kingsly because I knew he would send me the money to make this trip. I have not been able to work since my plane accident, and I could not have done this without his help." Alberto said, laughing.

Alberto picked up his sleeping bag and backpack and stepped onto the shore. I sat there motionless, under the brightly-lit sky, and a myriad of thoughts swirled around my head. I wasn't sure what to do next, but at the moment I had few options.

Alberto was already asleep when I stepped onto the bank – a solid gold necklace clasped around his neck, and the barrel of a Colt service revolver poking out from under his backpack.

A half-hour passed and I was still awake. I decided to get up and walk over to the *Mariana* and look for my pack of Camel cigarettes. Pepi was awake, his eyes focused on the forest underbrush.

Pepi awake? That's odd, I thought.

I lit up a cigarette and heard a faint sound – like the sound of Velcro being pulled apart.

Seconds later, I heard it again – louder this time.

*I heard a faint sound behind me – like the sound
of Velcro being pulled apart.*

I turned to look but saw nothing. Pepi seemed agitated and I crouched to stroke his head, and he strained his neck to look around me – behind me, in the direction of Alberto.

The silence was shattered by the primal scream of a man whose life was in mortal danger. I spun around, and in the moonlight saw a huge spider, hovering above Alberto – its front legs flailing in the air and jerking Alberto's body backward toward the dark jungle underbrush.

I ran towards the creature, waving my hands, and shouting wildly. The giant arthropod stood three feet on its haunches, its red beady eyes glowing like lasers. Alberto wasn't moving, and I reached for the Colt that was laying in the sand and aimed it at the hideous monster.

I fired once, and the revolver made a clicking sound. I fired again and again, and the cylinder turned and clicked six times. The gun was fully loaded, but the Colt would not discharge.

A blinding white light filled the forest canopy, and I could see a woman holding a baby, gliding slowly and silently toward me. To my left came a dozen or more people, and to my right appeared the *Toromona* Chieftain.

I recognized the tribe's Matriarch as she walked slowly toward Alberto's lifeless body, and the monstrous spider moved aside. She bent over and removed the gold necklace from Alberto and placed it around the Chieftain's neck.

The villagers began to chant softly in unison, and the Chieftain turned and looked to me with eyes that glistened silver. He raised his spear, and in a booming, unearthly voice said, "Go, now!"

I stepped slowly backward toward the shoreline, and the villagers watched, and their haunting chant grew louder. I felt the water around my ankles and turned quickly toward the *Mariana*.

I stumbled my way to the back of the boat and pulled hard on the engine cord several times until it finally ignited. I slammed the engine into gear and steered the *Mariana* westward into the current.

Dawn soon arrived, and I reached for the black silk cloth that Alberto had so unceremoniously tossed aside into the boat's hull – a silk shroud that once veiled a crescent medallion that's value was far more than the mere price of gold.

The Amazon had revealed her truths and her treachery, her wisdom and her powerful magic.

She had shown me the way we had all once lived so many thousands of years ago – and how little has really changed.

Pepi was once again sleeping soundly, tucked safely away under the deck of *Mariana's* hull, and I began to feel the warmth of the rising sun against my back, as we both made our way back home.

—

ABOUT THE AUTHOR

Cole Townsend attended Wayne State University in Detroit MI and moved west in search of adventure in British Columbia, Canada. After stints as a commercial fisherman and logger, he settled in Vancouver to pursue a variety of interests, including his passion for writing.

SPIDER MOON: Curse of the Gold Crescent - is his debut short story that attempts to blur the line between fact and fantasy.